It Wasn't Me

JOANNA NADIN

ILLUSTRATED BY PAULINE REEVES

BLOOMSBURY EDUCATION
Bloomsbury Publishing Plc
50 Bedford Square, London, WC1B 3DP, UK

BLOOMSBURY, BLOOMSBURY EDUCATION and the Diana logo are
trademarks of Bloomsbury Publishing Plc

First published in Great Britain in 2018 by Bloomsbury Publishing Plc

A catalogue record for this book is available from the British Library

ISBN: PB: 978-1-4729-5555-5; ePDF: 978-1-4729-5556-2; ePub: 978-1-4729-5554-8

2 4 6 8 10 9 7 5 3 1

Printed and bound in China by Leo Paper Products, Heshan, Guangdong

To find out more about our authors and books visit www.bloomsbury.com
and sign up for our newsletters

Chapter One

Alfie Braithwaite was always in trouble.
If the microwave exploded, Dad knew it
had to be Alfie.

If a goat appeared in the garden shed,
Mum knew it had to be Alfie.

If the cat, Caractacus, turned a strange shade of orange, Alfie's big sister Daisy knew it had to be Alfie.

But Alfie swore it wasn't him. "It's Dave," he insisted.
"Who's Dave?" asked Mum.
"The terrible gremlin," said Alfie.

"And where, exactly, does Dave live?" asked Dad.

"I've told you before." Alfie sighed. "In my sock drawer."

"Seriously?" said Daisy. "And I suppose he's green with purple eyes and an enormous wart on the end of his nose."

"No," said Alfie. "He's purple with green eyes and the enormous wart is on his bottom."

"Oh, Alfie," said Mum.

"Pull the other one," said Dad.

"Liar, liar, pants on fire!" yelled Daisy.

"I'm not lying!" said Alfie.

But he was. And he didn't stop lying either.

When Alfie mixed fourteen plastic horses into the cake Dad was baking, he blamed Dave.

When he gave one of Daisy's shoes to the dog next door, he blamed Dave.

And when he used up all of Mum's best perfume for a potion to make Caractacus disappear, he blamed Dave. "It really was him," he said. "If only you'd got here a minute earlier, you'd have seen him." "You're such a… a flapjack!" said Daisy.

"Next time you try it, it will be no pudding for you," said Dad.

"If you carry on lying, one day Dave really will show up, and then you'll be sorry," said Mum.

Like that will ever happen, Alfie thought to himself.

But do you know what? One sunny Monday morning in the summer holidays, it did.

Chapter Two

Alfie had just woken up and was
wondering what dastardly deeds to
do with his day when he heard a
commotion coming from his wardrobe.

That will be Caractacus, he thought.
I must have forgotten to let him out.
And grumbling to himself he trudged
to the cupboard, opened the door, and
saw that his sock drawer was rattling.

That's odd, thought Alfie. *I could have sworn I left him on the shoe self*. But he pulled the drawer open anyway. And that's when he saw him.

Not Caractacus at all, but someone smaller, and stranger, and smelling slightly of drains.

With a purple face and green eyes
and what looked suspiciously like an
enormous wart on his bottom.

"I- I- I-," stammered Alfie.

"I think what you're trying to say,"
began the little man, "is hello, Dave,
nice to meet you."

Alfie's mouth fell open.

"Don't do that," said Dave, "You'll swallow a fly. Now come on, we've got meddling to do."

"M-meddling?" managed Alfie.

"Of course!" cried Dave. "Isn't that what you like best?"

"I... suppose," admitted Alfie.

"Then let's get started," said Dave.
And with that he hopped out of the
sock drawer and headed straight for the
kitchen, with Alfie hurrying worriedly
behind.

"What are you doing?" demanded Alfie when he saw Dave pushing eleven pairs of Dad's red socks into the washing machine along with Daisy's special swan costume for the big ballet show.

"It would look far better pink," said Dave. "Don't you think?"
Maybe," said Alfie. "But I don't think Daisy will agree."

Alfie was right.

"What have you done?" she wailed
when she went to try it on.

"But it wasn't me," Alfie insisted. "It
was Dave. It really was. He's behind the
vacuum cleaner if you don't believe me."

But when Daisy went to look, Dave was gone.

"Stop lying, Alfie," she said.

"I'm not," said Alfie crossly. "It's the absolute truth this time. Dave really did do it, and he really does have a wart on his bottom as well."

But no matter how much he protested, no one believed him, and that night he was sent to bed without his pudding. Worse, it was chocolate mousse, his third favourite.

"You'd better not try that again," he said to the sock drawer as he lay in bed. "Go back wherever you came from."

But Dave didn't go back.

Chapter Three

On Tuesday Alfie was minding his own business reading a comic and eating a packet of jammy biscuits when Dave appeared next to him.

"Ooh, a slot," he said eyeing the DVD player. "Biscuits fit nicely into slots, don't you think?"

Now, Alfie had often thought that jammy biscuits would fit nicely into the DVD slot, but he hadn't tried it, because he knew what Dad would say. "I don't think so," he said to Dave.

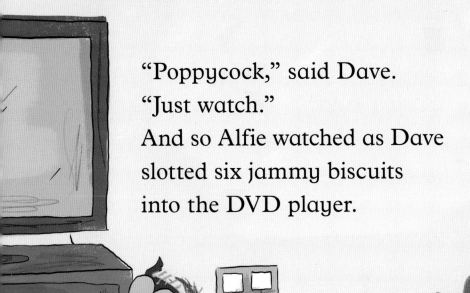

"Poppycock," said Dave.
"Just watch."
And so Alfie watched as Dave
slotted six jammy biscuits
into the DVD player.

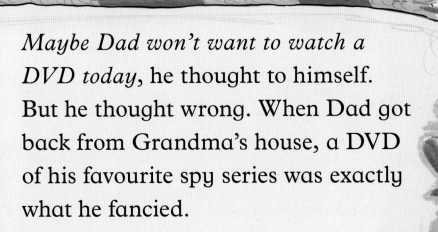

*Maybe Dad won't want to watch a
DVD today*, he thought to himself.
But he thought wrong. When Dad got
back from Grandma's house, a DVD
of his favourite spy series was exactly
what he fancied.

But when he tried to slide it into the DVD player, it wouldn't go, and when he opened the drawer he found a mess of jam and crumbs. "What in the name of Griselda Grout have you done this time, Alfie?" demanded Dad.

"It wasn't me," insisted Alfie. "It was
Dave. He's sitting in the plant pot if
you don't believe me."
But when Dad went to look,
Dave was gone.

"Stop lying, Alfie," said Dad.
"I'm not," said Alfie with
a sigh. "Really."

But that night he was sent to bed without his pudding again. And this time it was bananas and custard, his second favourite.

"Go home," he snapped at the sock drawer. "I wish I'd never thought of you."

Chapter Four

When Alfie woke the next morning, he opened the sock drawer straight away to find it empty. "Thank goodness!" he said. "Pudding for me today!"

But then he heard it: a terrible commotion from the kitchen that was part whirring, part splatting and part caterwauling from Caractacus.

Oh dear Alfie thought to himself. *That sounds like Dave.* And he scuttled downstairs to see what disaster Dave had dreamt up this time.

"You have got to be joking!" he exclaimed when he walked in. Because there on the kitchen counter was Dave with Dad's blender, which was spraying sticky pink liquid all over the room, including the walls, the ceiling, and Caractacus the cat.

"Nothing funny about a breakfast smoothie," said Dave. "Strawberry, yoghurt and sausage – my speciality." Alfie slammed the stop button on the blender – but not before he'd been showered in strawberry-flavoured sausage bits.

"What?" exclaimed Dave. "Don't tell me you've never thought of it."

Now the thing was, Alfie had thought about it, and often. But he hadn't actually ever done it. Because he knew what Mum would say. And he was right.

"Alfie!" shrieked Mum when she walked in. "Now what have you done?"

"I—" began Alfie.

31

But Mum interrupted. "And don't say 'It wasn't me' because your finger is on the button."

"Dave started it," said Alfie. "I was turning it off!"

"Go to your room," said Mum.

"Or rather, have a shower, and then go to your room."

"And don't think you'll be getting pudding later either," said Dad. "Because you've used up all the fruit."

"Don't tell me you were going to make..." began Alfie.

"... Strawberry glory," finished Dad.

Alfie hung his head. Strawberry glory
was his first favourite. And Dad
hardly ever made it as well because
the cream peaks were terribly tricky
to get just right.

Chapter Five

Alfie stomped off to wash the sausage out of his hair, and then slumped in his room in a sulk. *This has to stop*, he thought to himself. But how?

Talking to Dave didn't seem to work. And when he pulled open the sock drawer to try to catch him, Dave had disappeared, only to pop up on top of the bookshelves, and then in a shoe, and then outside the bedroom door,

which he knocked on loudly. But when
Alfie opened it, Dave ran off down
the landing.

No, Dave was far too wily for Alfie to
catch him in his bare hands. There had
to be a way though.

Alfie opened up Mum's computer and typed "how to get rid of a gremlin". Up popped all sorts of websites with all sorts of instructions.

Beryl from Bingley said it was best to douse them in damson juice. But Alfie didn't have any damson juice.

Colin from Cleethorpes said it was best to bop them on the head with a magic mallet. But Alfie didn't have a magic mallet.

Then he saw it: Gladys from Grimsby said the only way to get rid of a gremlin for good was to wash it in cold water, then it would sizzle for a second and disappear in a puff of purple smoke. And Alfie had cold water. Lots and lots of it. And he had something else too.

Alfie rummaged in his cupboard and found exactly what he was looking for: his Special Super Soaking Water Shooter, with pump action and shower effect. Then he remembered: Mum had banned it last summer after he super-soaked Caractacus and gave Daisy a shower effect with some mud.

But Alfie told himself that this was in a good cause and he made a promise too: if this worked, he'd never blame Dave for anything ever again.

And with the water shooter in his hand, and the promise in his head, off he went in search of Dave.

Chapter Six

The first place Alfie found Dave was sitting on Mum's best suit, which was laid out on the bed ready for her job interview.

Alfie aimed and fired, but by the time the water soaked the suit, Dave had long gone.

The next place he found him was dancing on Daisy's homework. Alfie aimed and fired, but by the time the water soaked the homework, Dave had long gone.

The next place he found him was
admiring Dad's prize painting, which
had only just dried. This time
Alfie was as quiet as quiet
could be. So that when he
took aim, Dave was still
staring at the
painting. And
when he fired,
Dave was still
staring at the
painting.

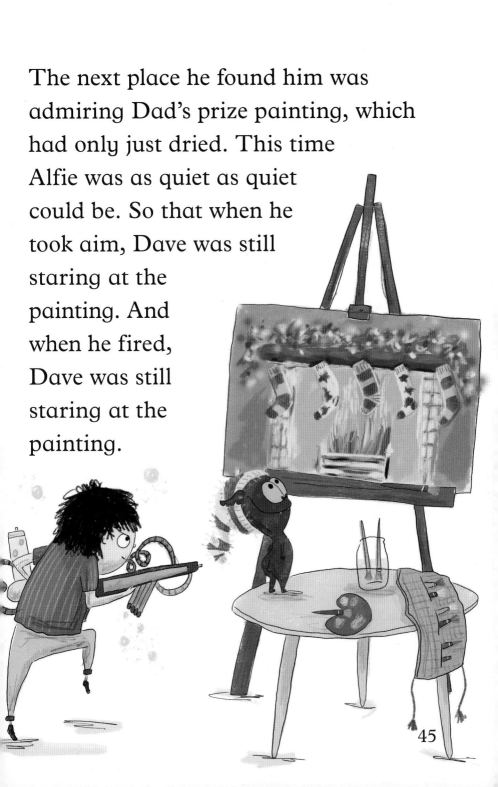

And when the water hit the canvas, Dave was still staring at the painting. But only for a moment. Because next he yelped. And he sizzled. And then he disappeared completely, just like Gladys said he would, leaving only a puff of purple smoke and a slight smell of drains.

"What on earth have you done to my painting?" demanded Dad when he walked in.

"And my suit?" sobbed Mum.

"And my homework!" Daisy stamped her foot.

"I suppose it was Dave again," said Dad.

47

"Actually," said Alfie. "It was me."
Dad looked puzzled.
Mum looked perplexed.
Daisy looked dumbfounded.
"Really?" they all asked.
"Really," said Alfie. "But I promise this
is the absolute last time."
And do you
know what?
It almost was.